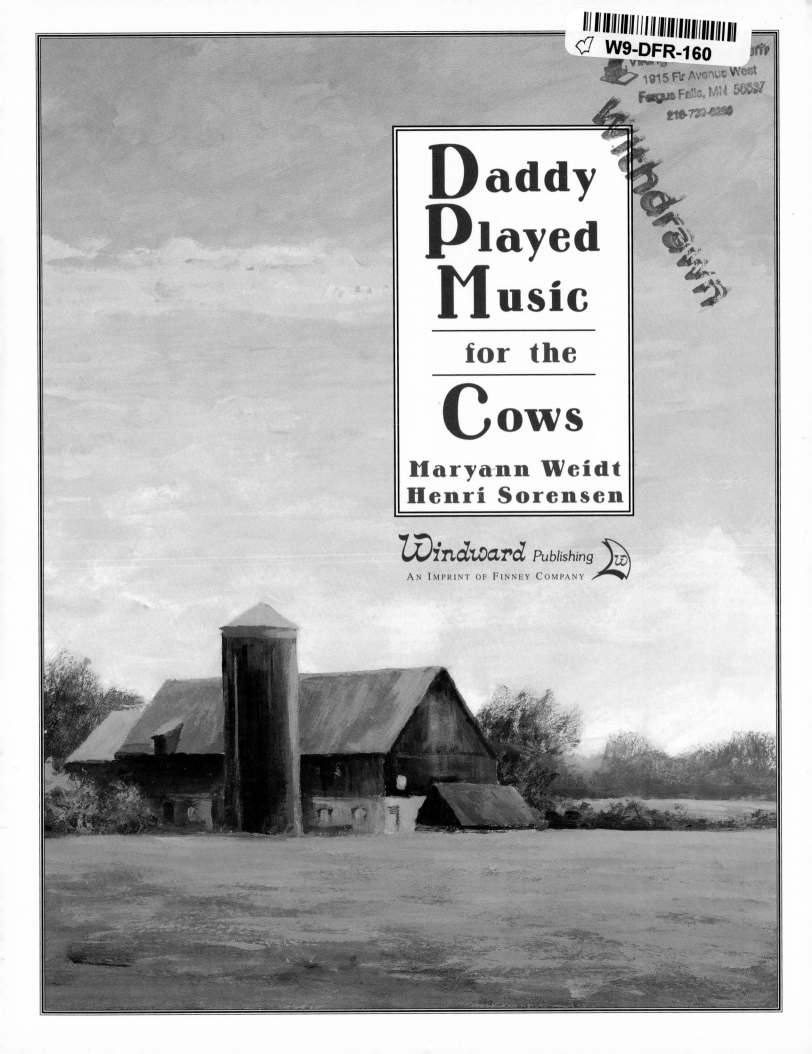

# Daddy Played Music for the Cows

Maryann Weidt
Henri Sorensen

**Windward** Publishing
AN IMPRINT OF FINNEY COMPANY

to my father, Andy Nieberle (1903-1957)
—MW

to my friends for more than 38 years,
Mogens Keblovszki and Palle Isbrandt
—HS

Special thanks to Susan Pearson, for listening and hearing a story.
Thank you Tom and Sonja Duesler and Helen and Dale Froemming,
two of our nation's valiant farm families—I salute you!

**Mama always said** I was born in the barn while Daddy played music for the cows. A bright red can full of seed corn was my rattle. It sang *kitch-ka-shoo, kitch-ka-shoo* when I shook it, while the cowboys sang on the radio and Daddy hummed along.

Mama set my playpen in the middle of the barn so I could listen to Daddy play music for the cows. When they strolled inside in slow motion, he picked me up and waltzed me down the aisle between them, patting their wide brown rumps and calling them by name— "Hey, Pearl Bailey, that's my girl....Come on, Queenie....Hello, Dolly"—as he nudged them into place.

The barn cats chased a sunbeam, and the kittens pushed their noses through my playpen bars. I shoved my nose out to meet them, and Daddy squirted warm milk at us while the radio sang *"yo-del-lay-hee-hoo."*

One day the playpen went to the attic, but Daddy still played music for the cows. The chickens danced a two-step in the corner of the barn. I squatted down to see where the eggs came from, and as I watched, out one popped. I caught it with both hands. The shell was soft and brown and warm. When I gave it to Mama, she tucked it into her apron pocket while she sang "Golden Rings" along with the radio.

Sometimes when Daddy played music for the cows, trumpet sounds filled every crack in the barn. Sleeping pigeons looked up from under the eaves. The mourning doves sang *coo-ooh, coo, coo-coo* as they flew down from the rafters, picked bits of corn off the floor, and flew away. I chased after them, laughing, but never caught more than the feathers they dropped.

While Daddy scooped manure from behind each cow, Mama spread hay beneath them. "It's all right, Dolly," she crooned. Dolly nodded and swayed, her hot breath coming in time to the music, as someone on the radio sang about the moon.

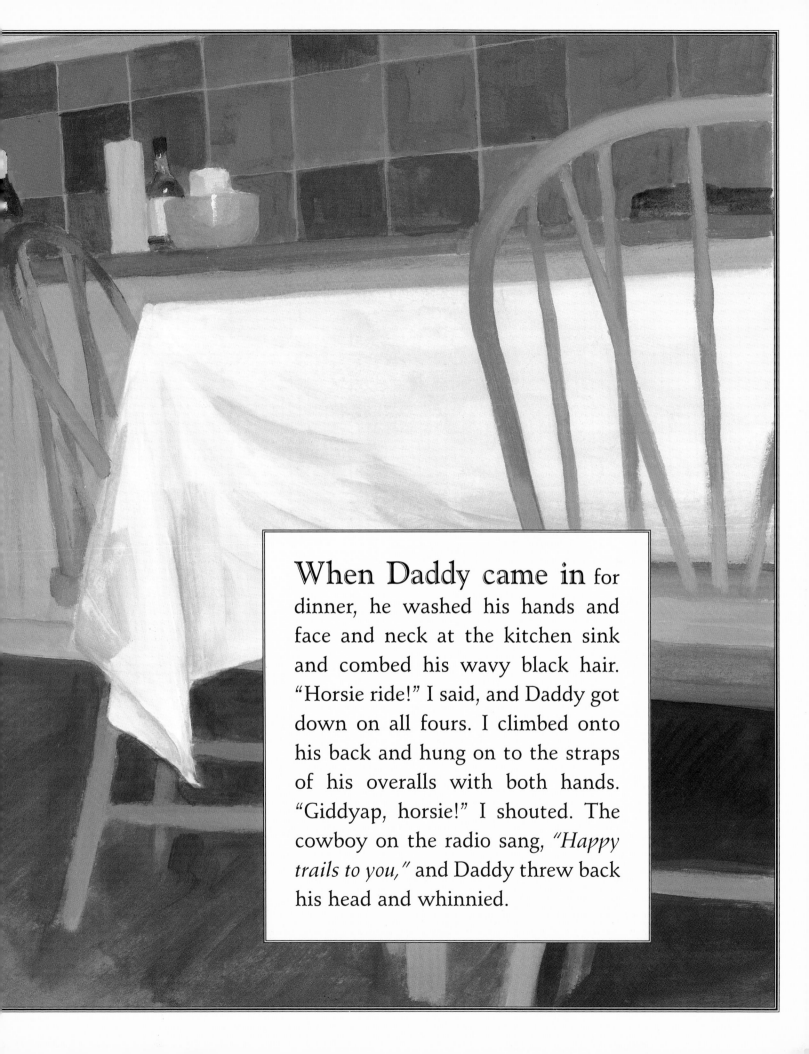

When Daddy came in for dinner, he washed his hands and face and neck at the kitchen sink and combed his wavy black hair. "Horsie ride!" I said, and Daddy got down on all fours. I climbed onto his back and hung on to the straps of his overalls with both hands. "Giddyap, horsie!" I shouted. The cowboy on the radio sang, *"Happy trails to you,"* and Daddy threw back his head and whinnied.

On my first day of first grade, I heard the cowgirls singing as I climbed off the bus and ran up the driveway. I changed my clothes as fast as I could, then raced for the barn. "Daddy!" I shouted. "I can read! Now I have to learn to yodel!"

**All that year** I listened to the cowgirls and tried to yodel just like them. I yodeled on the school bus. I yodeled when I fetched the cows from the pasture. I whirled and twirled and sang and yodeled and danced the chicken two-step down the center of the barn. *"Yo-del-lay-hee, yo-del-lay-heeee-hoooo."*

**In second grade,** I worked on my daring circus act. While Mama and Daddy milked the cows, I climbed inside the silo and hung by my knees from the ladder till the smell of silage made me dizzy. Then, holding my nose with one hand, I waved my other to the crowd. Applause bounced up and down the tall, cool walls. A single sunbeam held me in its spotlight while Daddy turned the radio to *"Toe-ray-a-doe-ra!"*

Mama always told me, "Don't play in the haymow," but when Jackie Bonniwell dared me, I climbed to the top, grabbed the rope, and swung like Tarzan across the whole length of the barn. When I let go, I fell screaming into a feather bed of hay. I felt like I was tumbling along with the tumbling tumbleweeds.

For my eighth birthday party, my friends and I dressed up as cowgirls. In the barn, the radio played *"Git along, little dogies"* while we played hide-and-seek behind the cows. "It's okay, Queenie," I said. "It's my birthday."

When Mama called, "Cake and ice cream!" we joined arms, kicked our boots in the air, and danced across the yard, singing *"Whoopee ti-yi-yo."*

**When I was as tall** as Daddy's armpit, I climbed onto the tractor and he showed me which levers to push and which to pull. Then I drove the tractor while Daddy and Mr. Bonniwell and Jackie put up hay. We worked all day and into the night to get the hay up before the rain. The music in my head sang one song after another: *Toe-ray-a-doe-ra...Happy trails to you...Yo-del-lay-hee-hoooooo.*

"Run and get the cows," said Daddy when the last load of hay was in the barn. I slid down the path to where Dolly and Pearl and Queenie were waiting with the others. I patted their soft warm bellies. Then, as they followed me to the barn, I lifted my chin and sang to the raindrops.

Daddy hugged me and laughed. "You look like a wet little muskrat," he said, "just like the day you were born." The air smelled of wet cows and steaming manure. "Listen," said Daddy as he turned up the radio. A cowgirl was singing our favorite song. Daddy hummed along, his voice flat and happy, and I yodeled like I never had before, while Daddy played music for the cows.